Library and Archives Canada Cataloguing in Publication

Cole, Kathryn, author
Never give up : a story about self-esteem /
by Kathryn Cole ; illustrated by Qin Leng.

(I'm a great little kid series)
Co-published by: Boost Child Abuse Prevention & Intervention.
ISBN 978-1-927583-60-9 (bound)

1. Self-esteem in children—Juvenile fiction. I. Leng, Qin, illustrator
II. Boost Child Abuse Prevention & Intervention, publisher III. Title.

PS8605.O4353N49 2015   jC813'.6   C2014-908041-7

Boost Child Abuse Prevention & Intervention gratefully acknowledges the generous support of Rogers Communications for funding the development and publication of the Prevention Program Series. Rogers Communications is an important partner in our efforts to prevent abuse and violence in children's lives.

Second Story Press gratefully acknowledges the support of the Ontario Arts Council and the Canada Council for the Arts for our publishing program. We acknowledge the financial support of the Government of Canada through the Canada Book Fund.

Published by
Second Story Press
20 Maud Street, Suite 401
Toronto, Ontario, Canada
M5V 2M5
www.secondstorypress.ca

Never Give Up

A story about self-esteem

written by Kathryn Cole
illustrated by Qin Leng

Second Story Press

Nadia watched the shiny new bike lean this way and that way. Shaun's tongue stuck out between his teeth as he struggled to stay balanced on the seat. He looked a little flustered.

The front wheel swung right and then left. It looked like the bike was taking Shaun for a ride, instead of the other way around.

Nadia forgot about the new skipping rope she had with her. She could practice later. She waved as Shaun wobbled past. To her surprise, he was still using training wheels.

He's not very good at that, she thought.

She sat down on the same grassy slope where her dad had taught her how to ride her own bike a whole year ago. Nadia was still watching when Kamal, Joseph, and Lin arrived on their bicycles with Lin's big brother, William. They noticed Shaun's training wheels too. It wasn't long before they were all making fun of him.

"Hey, little boy! Did your mommy take your tricycle away?" shouted Kamal.

"I've seen circus clowns ride better than that," added Joseph.

Lin nudged her brother, and they laughed so hard they were doubled over.

Shaun tried to ignore them. He looked even more flustered, but he kept going – until one of the training wheels hit a stone. The bike fell over. So did Shaun. Howls of laughter drifted across the park.

Nadia didn't know what to do. Shaun was her friend, and she wanted tell the kids to stop being so mean. But with four against one, she was afraid to say anything.

Shaun got up and wiped the scrape on his knee. It stung, but he picked up his bike and got back on. *Don't give up*, he told himself. *You can do this.*

Shaun tried again…and again. And again. Joseph, Lin, and Kamal laughed hard each time he crashed. And each time he crashed, Shaun ignored them and tried again. Pretty soon, the kids grew tired of teasing Shaun and followed William away. Joseph popped a wheelie as he left.

Nadia felt terrible. She picked up her rope and tried to practice skipping, but today she was even worse than yesterday. With every crash she heard, she tripped. Finally, she decided to go and talk to Shaun.

"I'm sorry they hurt your feelings," she told him.

"Doesn't matter," he said. "At least you didn't join in."

"It matters a lot. I should have helped." Nadia hung her head. "Are you okay?"

"Yes. And do you know what? I may not be good with bikes, but I can run fast and jump rope, and read, and…and do all sorts of things! Do you know why? It's because I never give up. They can laugh, but I'll end up riding this bike yet."

An idea was beginning to grow in Nadia's head. "Will you be here tomorrow?" she asked.

"Sure. If you bring the Band-Aids, I'll bring my bike." Shaun tried to smile, but his bumps and scrapes were hurting too much.

Maybe I'll bring something better than Band-Aids, thought Nadia.

At home, Nadia ran straight to her father. "Daddy," she said, "I need your help." She told him the whole story. When she finished she was in tears. "I was too afraid to stop them, so I just sat there like a lump. Shaun kept trying, and the kids kept laughing. It was awful."

"And now you don't feel like a good friend."

Nadia shook her head.

"Well, that makes me sad because how you feel about yourself is very important. What can we do to make this better?"

Nadia sniffled once or twice then told her dad about her idea.

"That's a great plan!" he said. "Of course I'll help. First, let me call Shaun's parents and see what they say."

Nadia felt a bit better. She crossed her fingers and made a wish: *Please let my idea work.* She would take some Band-Aids, just in case….

Shaun was already at the park when Nadia and her dad arrived. "What's the tool box for?" he asked.

"Well, when I was learning to ride my bike, Daddy said it was time to let the training wheels go. I was afraid, but he showed me how to keep my balance."

"What do you say, Shaun?" Nadia's dad asked. "Should I remove your training wheels?"

"Okaaay…. I mean…sure. I mean, yes. Yes, please!"

Nadia clapped her hands and jumped up and down. Shaun tightened his helmet.

In no time the training wheels were off. Nadia's father took the bike to the top of the grassy slope where Nadia had sat the day before. He told Shaun what to do.

"Sit on the bike and hold your feet out to the sides just above the ground. They are going to be your new training wheels. If you tilt a bit, push back up with your toes. At the bottom, put both feet down as you come to a stop. Got it?"

Shaun nodded, and before he knew it, he was coasting down the gentle hill. He only had to push once or twice with his toes before he came to a stop. He could hardly believe it!"

"Try again!" shouted Nadia. And he did. Again and again.

Soon Shaun didn't have to touch the ground at all. He felt good about himself.

"You're ready to put your feet on the pedals," said Nadia. "Don't push. Just leave them there. When you roll to a stop, put your feet down like before."

Shaun took a deep breath and followed Nadia's instructions. He got to the bottom without falling. He was so excited, he didn't see Lin, Kamal, and Joseph watching with their mouths open. But Nadia did, and she felt great. Nobody was laughing at Shaun now.

On Shaun's last trip down the hill, he kept his feet on the pedals, but as he slowed down at the bottom, he started to push. The wheels turned, the bike picked up speed, and without a wobble or a tilt, Shaun was riding his shiny two-wheeler! Cheers went up behind him – and in front of him. He felt like a king.

Nadia ran down the hill with her new skipping rope. "Now you can help me!" she said. "Daddy, will you turn the rope with Shaun so he can tell me how to run in? He's great at skipping."

"Gee, I don't know," said her father, shaking his head. "I was never very good at this."

Shaun and Nadia laughed. "Never give up!" they shouted.

"Here. Let me show you," came a voice. It was Lin. Behind her stood Joseph, William, and Kamal.

Before long, everybody was playing together. Shaun cheered each time Nadia ran in without tripping. And when her dad took a turn and fell, they all helped him up.

"I have just what you need, Daddy," Nadia said, offering him a Band-Aid for his scraped elbow. "There you go. Now try again!"

For Grown-ups

About Self-esteem

Self-esteem is a feeling of self-worth. It is how children "feel inside" about themselves. When children participate in activities that build on their strengths, it helps them to develop a sense of confidence and an appreciation of their abilities. Recognizing their efforts and accomplishments helps maintain their self-esteem and also encourages them to keep trying. Children who feel good about themselves are more likely to develop positive relationships and less likely to be mistreated in their interactions with others.

Parents can support their children to develop self-esteem:

- **Love them:** Show children they are loved and accepted by expressing affection and spending time together.

- **Play with them:** Create a safe, secure environment, encouraging children to explore the world around them.

- **Respect them:** Have realistic expectations, fostering positive experiences and success.

- **Appreciate them:** Accept children as individuals, reinforcing their strengths and abilities. Look for opportunities to talk about things that make them feel proud of themselves.

- **Talk with them:** Use positive ways to guide their behavior, treating all children in the family fairly.

- **Listen to them:** Children need to feel that they are contributing participants to the conversation in order to feel valued and respected; two key ingredients of self-esteem.